OF INFIDELS AND INFIDELITY

OF INFIDELS AND INFIDELITY

Manju Dhall

ZORBA BOOKS

ZORBA BOOKS

Publishing Services by Zorba Books, 2019
Website: www.zorbabooks.com
Email: info@zorbabooks.com

Copyright © Manju Dhall

Print Book ISBN: 978-93-88497-73-2
eBook ISBN: 978-93-88497-74-9

Zorba Books Pvt. Ltd.(opc)
Gurgaon, INDIA

*All women who have carried
the flag of women's rights*

Contents

1. Zurich 1
2. Atormin 11
3. Begum 15
4. A Perfect Relationship 33
5. The Courtyard 45
6. The House on Nawab Yusuf Road 57
7. The Ashram 71

Zurich

Some of us think holding on makes us strong,
but sometimes it is letting go.

—*Herman Hesse*

The check-in at Heathrow was crowded. And yet it was strangely quiet, unlike the persistent din at airports back home with its loud unabated announcements. They stood silently in the queue. She was lost in her thoughts, a nervousness creeping through her body as if something would suddenly give way. She needed to be alert. On the other hand, she was not really in control of herself. It was a decision that was guiding her. There were three passengers ahead of them. She watched as the young woman at the counter presented her passport to the airline official. The official smiled at her and the young woman smiled back. Now what could be so funny for both of them? Check in is usually so businesslike and precise. Her thoughts wandered and suddenly she found it was her turn. Her heartbeat quickened as she presented both their passports and e-tickets.

Abhijit put their bags on the belt. The passports were being examined. She turned to Abhijit and said, I'm really parched. I'll take care of this. Could you please get me a drink?'

1

'Are you sure you can manage?'

'Of course, it's all done as it is.' The turmoil inside her subsided somewhat as she watched Abhijit saunter away to get her a drink. She turned back and said,

'Could you give me a window seat please?'

Once in the aircraft, she was relieved to have settled down in her corner. She placed her handbag on the floor by the window, buckled in and looked out. It was a bright sunny morning and all she could see was the tarmac with numerous planes parked at the gates. A sense of relief swept through her. Now she could busy herself by looking at the world outside. She didn't dare look at Abhijit, sitting right next to her. He had picked up a newspaper from the Business class as they walked through the aircraft and some news had his undivided attention.

She shuddered at the memory. It was on their honeymoon that she first came face to face with the realization of who she had married. In that moment lay the greatest tragedy of her life to discover in the first week that she had made a huge mistake. It was a beautiful morning. She had woken up to find the sun streaming into the room. Abhijit was fast asleep. She got out of bed carefully, tiptoed across the room to the bathroom. When she emerged, he was still sleeping. Pulling her robe tighter across her ravished body, she opened the door to pick up the newspaper from the floor. Boring headlines, no news could rival the excitement of the first few days of married life, the togetherness, lying in each other's arms, the intense passion of the nights. And then something caught her eye. Her boss was leaving to join a multinational firm in Paris. She turned to the business page for any more details and as she turned the page, she saw Abhijit awake and looking at her intently. She smiled weakly and muttered a good morning. She continued to read the newspaper.

'Hey, can I have the newspaper?' She looked up from the paper, smiled mischievously and said, 'Come and get it, Mr. Rai.'

'How dare you speak to me like this?' He hollered at her and the next moment he jumped out of bed, yanked the newspaper from her hand and pushed her roughly against the couch. She was thunderstruck, speechless with fear, incredulous that Abhijit should be speaking to her in this manner as she crouched in the corner of the couch. It was as if she sat there a good part of her life. The morning seemed endless. She sat motionless, unable to move, or even think. What was happening to her? Where was she? Was this her newlywed husband? Did she do anything wrong that brought on such a response from Abhijit? She couldn't find any answers in her state of shock.

It was after a very long time that she moved from the couch. She found that he was sitting on the balcony reading the newspaper. She moved slowly into the bathroom, took a shower, got into her jeans and a warm jersey and walked out of the room without saying a word. The lobby smelt fragrant with fresh flowers.

The receptionist wished her a cheery, 'Good morning, Mrs. Rai' and she nodded, not forgetting to smile at the unsuspecting girl. She walked into the bracing mountain air. The touch of cold on her face jolted her into consciousness of where she was. She walked out of the gate on to the path that led to the main road that led to the golf course on the hillside on both sides of the road. Walking briskly, she let her body awaken from the stupor to which it had succumbed. Her mind was still confused as she tried vainly to understand Abhijit's retaliation to her playfulness.

When she returned to the hotel room, she found Abhijit still on the balcony. On seeing her, he hurried across the room, took her in his arms in a tight embrace as he muttered profuse apologies into her ear. Her reaction was quiet submission, once again failing to analyze his behaviour. The rest of the days were spent, outwardly normal and pleasant. But there was fearfulness in her soul and on unguarded moments she would study Abhijit's face and mannerisms very carefully, hoping to find some answers there for her self. There were no more incidents till they returned home to start a life of domesticity together.

But the incident on the honeymoon was the precursor to a life of total submission to her husband. She discovered his palpable rage as it simmered in their lives, reducing her to the role of a traditional woman, with an unquestioning attitude to his many moods. Abhijit's disapproval of everything she did was her undoing. She began to suffer a fear psychosis, being alert to his every expression, always nervous whether he approved or not. It was difficult to be carefree and casual in Abhijit's presence. She fell into a routine of scanning his face when he returned from work, always on guard.

The years went by. She found refuge in her work but was allowed little freedom apart from office hours. She brought in a hefty pay cheque which was very valuable to their existence. The babies came and she immersed herself in the joy they brought. The demands on her time were an escape from the insistent questions that troubled her. Relationships didn't matter to her anymore. Was there a relevant relationship between her and her husband? Her mind and heart questioned the validity of this lifelong alliance and could come up with no satisfactory answers.

But there were moments of utter desolation when she could not find consolation in her present. She felt with a numbing feeling that she had let herself down. What was she thinking? Whatever happened to her beauty and intelligence? Why was she not the architect of her own destiny? She had allowed her life to drift, swept away by the current, at times peaceful and tempestuous at other times. These conflicting periods had made her very unsure of what she really wanted. Her submission was in fits and starts. The defiance brought more grief so there were moments when she just let things be, passed her days in a fitful consciousness. It was a vague existence. She moved around doing household chores busily, occupying her days with the mundane and dutiful tasks that somebody has to do and that left her little time to pause and think.

When she was young she was very teary-eyed. She would cry at the slightest. There were times when she was so overcome by a situation that she couldn't control herself. Her sobs would wrack her body and soul till she exhausted herself. And then she would calm down. The storm had passed. But now her tears were unabated. Her tears would flow anywhere, at home, in public places, while driving. Once when she was going to see her parents, she settled into her seat in the train and the thought of the children made her cry uncontrollably. It was embarrassing. She averted her gaze from the other passengers, crouched in the seat and looked out of the window till her neck ached. Many times she would cry while driving, unable to control her self, until her vision became cloudy and she would just let the tears flow, not caring who was looking or who was curious.

She lived at two levels. For external appearances, she was an excellent housewife and mother, accomplishing each task with a willingness that was natural to her. Work brought her blessed enjoyment, an opportunity to spend time away from home, associating with her colleagues that brought such peace and calmness to her mind. At work she was considered a liberated woman, with excellent skills of managing a perfect work-life balance. But the inner woman was always in turmoil, a turmoil born of her inability to take her own life's decisions. She felt cloistered, hemmed in by a cocoon that she had woven around herself. While it was of her own making she found it very difficult to break free. She reveled instead in obedience, of giving in to every whim and fancy of her family. She also found peace there. Seeing the children grow up into two responsible, bright young people she was full of pride as they found their life's work and both went away to the United States. Kavita left for Columbia to do an advanced course in journalism. Six months later Anshul joined Microsoft in Seattle. She missed them greatly but the satisfaction of having done a job well was her reward. She immersed herself with more intensity into her own work.

She had one friend at work in whom she had confided. Bhavani understood her predicament and often chided her for being so weak-kneed. And then came the offer of a coveted job in an organization in Switzerland. Bhavani was excited about it and argued with Kamini about not missing the opportunity of a lifetime. Kamini was torn with indecision and the possibility of being at last the woman she secretly longed to be. For her life was at the crossroads where all she needed to do was to muster the courage inwardly to take her own decision. She, however, permitted herself to be badgered into doing all the paperwork for the application despite her remonstrations.

A few months later Abhijit came home one day from work and announced that he had a conference in London to attend. Whether it was the departure of Kavita and Anshul or some softening towards her, he told her she should take off from her work and accompany him to London. She was surprised but agreed willingly. There were still four weeks to go. She told Bhavani about it and Bhavani dropped a bombshell by saying that she should join them in Zurich on this trip.

The sadness of London. The loneliness of sitting on the steps of the British Museum by herself. As she turned into Gower Street now up to where the Law department was she saw that it wasn't there any more. Wading her way across Russell square she was overcome by an overwhelming sense of sadness, the sadness that had been under her skin all these years, a loneliness suffused with an utter sense of confusion. Then she had asked herself the question, 'What am I doing here?' Nothing had changed. She still strode the streets of London with a lonely heart, a heart aching for the touch of another, the warm arms of a loved one. All her life she had sought this companion but she was always left with her own thoughts. It is a dangerous thing to be left alone with your own thoughts.

The flight to Zurich was uneventful. She had her full snack to give herself much needed energy. When they landed in Zurich they hurried towards the gate to take their flight home.

When they reached the gate she placed the carry on bag on the x-ray machine and turned around to face Abhijit behind her.

'You carry on. There's still time. I'll just go to the washroom before boarding. It's a long flight ahead and I want to stretch my legs before boarding,' she said calmly.

'You better hurry. There's not much time,' he said impatiently.

She turned around and walked across the hall towards the toilets. She didn't look back as she walked past the toilets and hurried on. She checked the signs above for immigration and it pointed towards the left. Her steps became faster with a tightening in the calves of her legs as she turned the corner and was lost to the view. It was going to be a fairly long walk to immigration. The sprawling modern airports make you walk miles to get anywhere. She stood at the platform waiting for the sky train that would take her to Immigration. As the doors of the sky train closed she lost her balance suddenly but steadied herself by grabbing the nearest pole.

Finally, she reached the Immigration desks. Fortunately, there was only one Arab woman with a headscarf ahead of her. When her turn came the immigration officer checked her passport, looked at her and asked her how many days she planned to spend in Zurich. She answered that she would stay only two days. He made a few clicks on his computer and returned her passport. As she passed through immigration she felt her heart pounding with fear, excitement and uncertainty. Shrugging these weakly she picked up her solitary bag that lay near the baggage beltway. All the other passengers had taken theirs and were probably already on their way home or to their particular destinations. As she walked out of the exit doors wheeling her bag behind her she came into contact with the cool, fresh, bracing air. She hailed a taxi, got into it with still weak determination and said,

'Please take me to the Zurich Hauptbahnof.'

Atormin

It was a sultry afternoon. The air was heavy, languorous and debilitating. After lunch she felt lazy and lay down in the kids' room that adjoined their bedroom. She had nothing much to do. She shut her eyes and tried to take a nap. But sleep eluded her. She could hear Arun in the other room. He was already packed for the journey. He was going away, far away, to distant lands, an assignment that he didn't mind taking up because it was lucrative.

From where she lay she could see her bed but the rest of the room was hidden from sight. For a long time, she lay in a kind of lazy stupor, flitting between a state of semi-consciousness and wakefulness. And then the phone rang. She heard Arun answer the phone and heard him say,

'Where have you been all day? I've been waiting for your call all day.' And then silence as he listened to the person at the other end.

'I have to see you before I leave. Have to leave for the airport at nine thirty. Come with me to the airport.'

Silence again as he listened.

'O.k. I'll meet you in the evening. At the Metro theatre. In the parking. At seven thirty. Don't be late.'

Maya lay still, unmoving. What did she hear? Her heart stopped beating. She couldn't believe her ears.

11

She felt an emptiness overtaking her as if her blood had stopped flowing in her veins. She lay with her eyes shut, not stirring at all. She heard Arun walk through the room. She still did not get up from the bed. Her mind was in a turmoil. Who was he talking to? Why this rendevouz at seven thirty in the parking lot of a theatre? Who was he going to meet? He was leaving that same evening and yet he was going to meet someone and in a parking lot?

It was a bolt of lightning that hit her. He was going to meet a lover; someone he had been waiting to hear from. It was someone he wanted to say goodbye to. It was a subterfuge. After a long time, she got up. It was teatime. She went into the kitchen to make tea. Her legs wouldn't carry her. She couldn't think straight. Her mind was in a total haze. As she brought the tea for everyone into the living room, she looked around her home. The living room was a modest but pretty room. The carpets, the few precious artefacts they had acquired, the silk drapes were all that she had put together to make her home beautiful within their means. But at this moment the room stifled her. Her insides were trembling. While she went around calm on the exterior, the trembling inside her body was a totally new sensation. It unsettled her. Her world had crashed; she did not exist anymore. Her consciousness was as if she was a ghost. Till she heard Arun say,

'I need my blood pressure medicine. Must get Atormin before I leave.' She heard him and the import of the words hit her like a boulder.

After that she watched him keenly. She watched every move of his without as much as a word from her unless spoken to. She saw the liveliness of his step. She heard the keenness in his voice. She saw his face relax. It was a new Arun she was watching, a younger, happier Arun. More relaxed, more youthful with an unnamed excitement of anticipation in him. This was the anticipation of meeting someone who made his blood race. She liked the Arun she saw but the thought brought with it a load of sadness. This Arun was not meant for her. She saw a carefree Arun, not the serious man she had a relationship with.

Her eyes sought the watch again and again. Her mind sought a dangerous confirmation of what she suspected.

She tried to busy herself with inconsequential things. She put away the washing. She went to her sister-in-law's room to put away their clothes. She asked her mother-in-law what she would like for dinner. And then she noticed the time. She quickly left to look for Arun. She went into the bedroom. He was not there. She peeped into her bathroom. She looked all over, in the garden. No sign of Arun. And then she noticed the empty garage. The car and Arun were gone.

She was delirious with an unknown fear. She started trembling, a trembling she couldn't control. All her fears were confirmed. He had gone to keep his seven thirty appointment. It was twenty past seven. It would take him but a few minutes to reach. Like a woman possessed she walked out of the house, and into the square. Darkness had fallen. There wasn't a soul outside. She walked around with a blank mind. She couldn't think at all. She just walked till she tired herself out. With an unwilling heavy step, she walked into the house and just sat on a chair in the verandah. After what seemed an eternity the door opened and Arun walked in. She scrutinized his face. He looked happy and relaxed.

'Where did you go?' was all she managed to say.

'I went to get Atormin.' It was a matter of fact statement, barely giving away anything. Who could guess? He didn't know she felt half dead, with a trembling in her body that she couldn't explain.

'You won't come to the airport to see me off, will you?' It was a statement not to be contradicted. A friend came over to say goodbye to Arun and stayed for dinner. She was beside herself trying to muster up an effort to appear normal. The trembling would not ease or stop. In some time, he was gone, leaving her with the burden of a lifetime.

Begum

U nlike the cycle of nature that is so regular and certain. Look at this tree outside, she said, pointing to the leafy branch of the Neem beyond the window. There is a pattern to its existence, when it will bloom, when it will bear fruit and when it'll do its autumnal shedding. Human lives are most unpredictable. We are all creatures of accident. Our birth is an accident and so it proceeds the rest of our lives. We plan regardless of our circumstances, we attempt to soar against the wind, we choose our partners with a level head. But life, unforgiving life, takes over and buffets our days like nobody's business.

There was a persistent din at the party headquarters. There were groups of people all over in all the rooms. And the ubiquitous hangers on were the ones you had to reckon with. Will my contact be able to give me some information? Well, soon it turns out he is just cooling his heels there waiting for instructions from Shri Babulal Gupta, the supremo in this office, whether he should go ahead with the new strategy. I was also waiting to hear from the horse's mouth the choice of candidate for the Purana Bazaar seat. That it was to be a woman was certain. As it is the number of women parliamentarians was so dismal that there was great consternation in the rank and file of women in the party. When will women get justice in society and be noticed as individuals in their own right instead of being mere appendages?

I approached one of the desks and was instantly rewarded. Am I lucky, I asked myself? Because, there before me was the sole person I was unlikely ever to meet. She was known to be unapproachable, very powerful in the organization and the world within the party moved only at her behest. What was she doing at one of these plebeian desks? I recognized her at once, the attire and the bearing of one in authority. A cool grey sari with a deep blue woven border with a hint of a line of gold with a matching dull pink purple blouse that complimented the greyness of the sari. Her salt and pepper hair was tied in a loose bun, a bindi on her exalted forehead, a beady necklace going down the front, a steel watch on her right wrist, the other vacant. I was at once on my guard, remembering what Swati, my senior colleague had remarked about this power centre in the party.

'She doesn't entertain journalists at all. But the party spokespersons are briefed by her. Her word is law.'

I approached the desk a bit diffidently.

'What do you want?' She looked up from the file she was examining, her voice betraying a cocktail of irritation and authority.

I shuffled my feet and in a rather uncharacteristic timid tone of voice asked, 'Ma'am, I represent India News.' Why do people in authority have such a numbing effect on me? My career as a journalist was doomed if I didn't grow nerves of steel. I straightened my back, unobserved, because the lady had gone back to the papers before her.

'Has the party high command decided on the candidate for Purana Bazaar?'

Why do people in authority have such a numbing effect on me?

'You'll be better off asking the high command. Now, please go because I have work to do.'

I persisted. 'Ma'am, if I may ask, are you a contender too?' It was a suicidal question. She looked up, her eyes steely and yet entertaining the inevitable question.

'I don't like pesky reporters. Leave before I call security.'

That was the end of my tete e tete with her for the day.

I left timidly and found myself outside in the cool air, breathing in heavily to sustain my frayed nerves. But somewhere I was determined to know more about this remarkable woman who carried an aura of mystery about her. There was little gossip about her. Any reference to her was made in awe and with some trepidation with a lurking fear that you could get into trouble if you fished in troubled waters. You couldn't speak lightly about her. Rarely did any political persona ever carry so much mystery and respect. There was never any speculation about it either. She was more or less left alone and out of the gossip columns. It was the status accorded to royalty by good journalism.

The announcement of the Purana Bazaar candidate came three days later and the pictures of Kamla Tripathi shone out of all newspapers. It was a very prestigious seat for the All India Democratic Front and psephologists were agreed that the party that won the Purana Bazaar seat carried the elections to the assembly traditionally. But the buzz was more about the candidate who despite the authoritative reputation was virtually unknown to the general public. The media was agog with excitement to follow her campaign and how it would be planned. I was determined to follow her trail during the campaign and decided to broach the subject with my editor. There was a nagging and gnawing desire inside me to know more about this candidate and the circumstances that shaped her into the position of power without a public face.

How much do we know about any individual at all? It is not possible to get into the head of a person to find out how his stream of consciousness moves, whether it is quiet flowing or always skipping along in rapids. The other day I was face to face with a father who described how he gave up everything, including his job, to be with his bipolar son, to be his constant companion, to protect him against himself. The dad's dedication and devotion to this job he had assigned himself was exemplary. He was a quintessential father, leading a normal life of going to work and back with the family in the evenings. What were the newly awakened emotions in him that prompted him to change the course of his life? His satisfaction lay in the fact that his son led a normal life punctuated by periods of depression and uncertainty when the presence of his dad was like the presence of god shielding him from the ravaging effects of his own mind. The culminating words of the dad were, 'I became not only a better dad but a better person as well. I became a gardener, a writer, an actor. I learnt to be more tolerant, more giving and I was more satisfied with my life than if I'd been doing a nine to five job.'

The shrillness of the campaign was deafening as it gathered tempo day by day. The opposing candidate of the Progressive Party was a well known businessman of Purana Bazaar who hobnobbed with the shopkeepers

18

on a daily basis and had been doing that for decades. He was swaggering in his confidence that no one could challenge him in Purana Bazaar. And a woman? It was almost a laughing matter for him.

However, I was still waiting for Kamla Tripathi's campaign to begin. It had been days now after the announcement by AIDF and the excitement in me was palpable that I was to witness something out of the ordinary. Kamla Tripathi aroused the curiosity of a cat in me and I was very anxious to probe into her personal life and her antecedents. It was no easy task. For a public figure to be so mysterious was agonizingly strange and it compelled me to intensify my efforts to find out where she lived, about her background, her family and her political alliances.

I began following her when she would leave the party headquarters for home. It was several days and many different modes of travel to avoid detection that I was able to reach what I gathered would be her home in one of the quieter and upmarket neighbourhoods of the capital. One could hear dogs barking as the gate opened just enough to let in her car by the guard at the entrance. Enquiries at the party headquarters meant to be discreet were always frowned upon by everyone. Why this closely guarded secret? I meant to talk frankly with one of my colleagues.

My opportunity came when Himesh Prasad, who had been my mentor at India News, returned as the bureau chief after having spent eighteen months in the new southern capital where he had been assigned to open a new office for India News. We had become buddies as I trained for two years under his wings.

Himesh was very thorough in his work, brooked no slip shod excuses, and had very close contacts in all political circles. Besides his manner was suave and poetic with an ever smiling and laughing mien that endeared him to all he came into contact with. He had instilled a genre of journalistic ethics into me that was not to be ever compromised for the sake of sensationalism. I called him to welcome him back and said, 'Lets have dinner at the Kothi tomorrow. I have so much to tell you.'

Over burra kebabs and succulent seekhs, crisp nans and dal Himesh regaled me with stories of the aspirations of the CEO politician of the newly formed state who had a grand vision for the state. If only these were not confined to architectural proportions. What about the people and their needs? I was not impressed and what was bothering me was the lady and her story if Himesh could shed some light on it.

'You are preoccupied with something, Ram. What is it?'

'What can you tell me about Kamla Tripathi?'

'Oh, so that's it.' And in the next hour Himesh had me spell bound with the story of a remarkable woman who had several avatars, one bolder than the others. It was a narrative of intelligence, academic brilliance, superb performance at work and a charisma that few could deny if I were to believe Himesh as he unfolded her life's narrative to me.

'Kamla Tripathi was found by the Prime Minister on his visit to the United Kingdom. Her husband was posted as the Deputy High Commissioner in London. I was accompanying the Prime Minister only because I was the replacement for my editor who had fallen sick on the eve of the visit. This was about 15 years ago. We spent three days in London and it was at India House at the Reception that all eyes pivoted on Kamla Tripathi as she mingled among the guests. I still remember her as she meandered through the groups of people in her crimson silk sari, her stately figure erect, till she found herself in the PM's group. She was a beautiful woman nobody could ignore, not even the PM. Initial introductions over, the PM enquired whether she liked London despite the dreary weather. Kamla Tripathi replied that the weather went unnoticed as she had a lot of work. She was doing her Doctorate at the London School of Economics on the desirable imperatives of the welfare state. The PM was suitably impressed and having assumed power not too long ago and a number of initiatives the government intending announcing for the alleviation of poverty in India, he was drawn into a discussion with her. He led her to a corner where for the next half an hour he did not allow his aides to interrupt, so engrossed was he in what Kamla Tripathi had to say. Her talk with the PM was noticed by everyone in the room.'

'Her rise after that chance meeting with the PM was sudden, swift and meteoric, Himesh went on.' The Prime Minister invited her over for breakfast the next morning to continue their dialogue and offered her a position in the government as an expert. To turn down the PM would've been difficult but she found an easy option that she had to complete her thesis. She was also bowled over by her own confidence and daring in the way she spoke with conviction and a soft aggression. She had worked as a consultant after Business school wherever her husband was posted. She was an intellectual Everest so had no difficulty in finding some area of work as she accompanied her husband around the globe.'

My head was spinning with critical questions of how she became a political power centre. Himesh went on.

'A few years later after that chance meeting with the Prime Minister, she came back to the capital when her husband took voluntary retirement. It was reported that he would occupy himself with academic pursuits while she became a junior advisor in the main think tank of the establishment. From there she joined the party and worked behind the scenes mainly to prepare strategies for elections at various levels. She became the power centre to whom everybody turned including all the functionaries of the party, high and low. She confers with the Prime Minister and senior ministers, at the centre and the states.'

'What about her husband? What does he do?'

Himesh shrugged his shoulders and said, 'The focus has been on her. He is not seen anywhere with her. But it hasn't gone unnoticed that she operates alone. She is socially not active at all. There are no occasions where the two of them are seen together.'

'But doesn't the media hound her personal life since she seems to be the epicentre of power play?'

'There is some element of mystery surrounding her, Ram. She has become so powerful that some questions remain unanswered. I wouldn't want to stray into her personal life.'

The evening wore on in discussion revolving around the upcoming elections. But my mind was preoccupied with Kamla Tripathi. I was determined to find out about her personal life, her husband, her children if any. Why did her husband cut short his brilliant career? Surely not to accommodate his wife! Himesh noticed my unbelieving countenance and reproved me,

'Ram, surely, you're not going off the tangent! Beware, I'm warning you.'

'Does this mean you know something but won't share it with me?'

'On no, its not like that. I've heard rumours that I would not like to multiply. Let's leave it at that.'

I did not wish to displease Himesh with importunate queries any further. We parted company on a pleasant note by having paan at the famous paan shop outside the restaurant.

The next morning, I planted myself quite early, about 50 yards from her gate, and was instantly rewarded. Exactly at seven the gates opened and a tall handsome gentleman in shorts and a red t-shirt stepped out accompanied by a golden retriever and a young lad. As they walked towards me I noticed that the gentleman had a firm, purposive stride, obviously in good robust health. The young lad with him looked about 14 years old. As they went past I tried eye contact with the gentleman but he was too preoccupied to even notice me. The lad looked at me briefly but his lack of interest was due to the dog whose leash he was pulling even though the poor animal was trying to pee.

'Come on Zen. Come on Zen.' Zen was pronounced with an extra emphasis on the vowel, totally distorting the excellent name of the creature. They moved ahead pretty quick as the gentleman was walking in long strides with the boy and the dog scampering after him.

Sleepy and tired after my early morning rendevous, I turned the car around after a lapse of five minutes and drove in the same direction after them. I drove a bit slowly as I came closer to watch them enter the big community park. I parked the car outside the park and settled down to wait for when they would emerge from the park.

I woke up with a start and when I looked at my watch I realized I had succumbed to blessed tempting sleep for over an hour! This is futile, bumbling, unprofessional investigation, I told myself.

Undeterred, the next day I planted myself on a bench among some shrubs in the park close to the entrance. Soon, the party of three entered the park and went down the walking path among the daily veterans, joggers and others. I hurried after them, caught up and when my opportunity came, overtook the gentleman on his left. Looking back at his face I addressed him directly and said, 'You walk really fast.'

At first there was no reaction to my words, then a perplexed look, followed by a frown, bringing the brows together and at last a smile.

'Oh, yes, yes.' And he continued walking in his very decisive, measured steps, looking straight ahead, having summarily dismissed my interruption. Being new at this game I decided to withdraw and return home.

Meanwhile the election campaign was picking up steam with all the accompanying tumult of sloganeering, poster campaigns, loudspeakers blaring on rickshaws, and door to door visits, all strategies being used to persuade voters. Kamla Tripathi had not yet addressed the voter but her face on posters was everywhere. Her picture was a head turner in that it was a blend of beauty, charm and gravitas. Would the ordinary voter be influenced? Would her being a beautiful woman sway the voter? Would her gender be the critical factor? What would her speeches be like? I was very curious and waiting to hear her make her maiden political speech. What issues would she address? What would be the pillars of her platform? Its one thing wielding power behind the scenes but it is another story to get your hands into the dirt. And the dirt of politics can be stinging and abrasive!

I kept a close watch on every aspect of her election campaign and excitedly awaited her first political rally that she was to address on the Dusshera grounds. But at the same time I was curious to know more about her husband.

'I am not standing here before you to ask for your vote. I am here to ask for your support so that we can work together to build this country. I know the needs of the people for a better life. You need schools for your children, clean efficient hospitals to take care when you fall sick, sympathetic doctors to listen to you when you need them, clean water supply and uninterrupted electricity for your homes and businesses. You would like clean, safe neighbourhoods, and above all a responsive government that does not seem too far to approach.'

Standing tall behind the podium, dressed in an off white cotton sari with a green border, Kamla Tripathi was a study in confidence. Her voice as it went over the city ramparts was very clear and booming, without any pauses or interruptions. To the left was a large screen which showed her on the screen in full splendour. As the crowd watched and heard in awe this beautiful woman who spoke directly to them without any political rhetoric, I was wondering about the man in her life. She was long married but at this juncture when her political career was taking the next logical step, he was not present by her side. Was he not interested? Had he relinquished all in her favour? There were very many troubling questions that dogged me. I resolved to meet the threesome again in the park the next day. Kamla Tripathi's speech was well received and the entire media flashed it all evening.

The next morning, I pushed myself out of bed much against my wont to make it to the park in time. As I drove towards the park gate I could see them entering the park with the gentleman ahead of the others. I parked the car hurriedly and much to my chagrin was pulled up by an elderly gentleman for my tire having climbed the low hedge.

'These young people are always in a hurry, even early in the morning. Please watch where you're going.'

I couldn't care less as I knew I would have to sprint to catch up with them. I walked fast, almost running, jumping over the low hedges where the track didn't give way to me and not wanting to disturb the peace of the walkers around me. Yet I was the cynosure of all eyes around me, eyebrows raise in annoyance! What's the darned hurry, they seemed to say? Catching up with the gentleman I fell into step with him. Turning towards him I wished him good morning. No response.

Again I tried, 'How are you?' No response.

We kept walking side by side and I have to confess that I was almost out of breath keeping pace with him. He's annoyed at the uncalled for interruptions of a total stranger. But I was determined to solve the puzzle that was by now an obsession with me. We were now at the other end of the park and as we reached a small wooden bridge over a stream below and where there was place for only two abreast I said,

'Your wife gave a very powerful speech yesterday. It was very well received in the media. Congratulations.'

He turned towards me and I watched the indifferent expression on his face. There was no hint of any pleasure, irritation, or reaction to the compliment.

'Yes, Yes,' he said in a very matter of fact manner and simply walked on.

No, I was not going to give up. I followed him and in a tone of insistence said, 'Sir, how do you support her campaign? Do you advise her?'

'No, no,' he replied in a peremptory voice. 'No, no, no!' He looked upset and the lad hastened his step towards us and told me,

'Leave him alone.' And turning towards the gentleman said, 'Sahib, let's go home.' And before I could gather my thoughts they moved away quickly. The gentleman walked very fast in any case.

I returned to my apartment in a perplexed state of mind. I had failed to elicit any response from Kamla Tripathi's husband. The situation was becoming somewhat of a puzzle. Maybe he didn't reply because I had not introduced myself as a reporter. He may have then been compelled to say something but this total silence from a close of kin of a public figure disappointed me. I mustn't surrender. Instead I decided to intensify my efforts.

Kamla Tripathi's campaign gathered momentum. She was fast becoming a household name from a hitherto ivory tower position. The opposition found it difficult to project any negativity about her. Contrary to expectations of political pundits she impressed voters by a direct appeal and at times her searing yet polite criticism of other candidates found many hardliners simmering with anger. The exit polls gave her a clear margin over the others.

I let a week go by before I ventured again. A cool summer morning breeze had brought out residents to the park in large numbers even though it was quite early. Still somewhat groggy I sat on a bench about forty yards from the gate. Whoa! I felt I was blessed as I saw an addition to the party of threesome. Kamla Tripathi in a white salwar kurta accompanied the group. I was stunned. As they approached nearer, I got up and almost intercepting their way said cheerily,

'Good morning Ma'am. Such a pleasure to see you here.'

A look of thoughtfulness flipped across her face, her eyes looking for an answer.

'Who are you?' she said calmly though. The lad interjected,

'He's the man who spoke to sahib the other day.'

Kamla Tripathi's face by now was a picture of complete annoyance. I expected her to censure me. But she retained her composure and said,

'Aren't you the reporter from India Times? What are you doing here? Please don't disturb us.' The words were polite and inoffensive but the underlying tone was ominous. With nerves of steel and much against the advice of peers I persisted.

'I would like to interview sir. What role does he play in your election campaign?'

'You will do nothing of the sort.' She almost thundered in the peace and calm of the morning.

Turning round, she said, 'Let's go back home.' It was only the lad who obeyed her command. The dog looked quizzically at his mistress. Mr. Tripathi stood still till the lad nudged his elbow saying, 'Sahib, let's go.'

'Ma'am,' I started to say but her raised hand silenced me and I watched them walking rather briskly and purposefully toward the park gate from where they had come.

The encounter dampened my resolve as I felt a nagging discomfort about my observations. I didn't want to broach the subject with Himesh for fear of being reprimanded. The election day drew nearer. There was excitement all around. The turnout at the polling was better than expected and the long serpentine lines of women voters confirmed the predictions of the exit polls about a thumping victory for Kamla Tripathi. She won by a wide margin trouncing entrenched politicians in her maiden election. The newspapers were full of her achievements, and there were several references to her antecedents as well as write ups about her position in the party. Of course there were innumerable stories regarding the berth she was likely to occupy in the ministry. I have to admit that I was careful but I couldn't restrain myself in one of my write ups from making a reference to her husband as an ex-diplomat and whether he played a role in her political life. My questions had remained unanswered. I decided to visit her home again.

This time I didn't lay in wait outside but rang the bell. A guard in uniform opened the gate and enquired who I wanted to see.

'I want to meet Madam Tripathi,' I said, handing him my card.

After what seemed like an age the gate opened and he let me in. We walked towards the verandah where Kamla Tripathi stood. It was only 8:30 in the morning but she was all dressed to leave for work. She did not ask me to sit down. Neither did she return my greeting. She looked very grave.

'You have been pestering my family and I could take some strict action against you.' She paused.

'But you are young and as a journalist you think you have the credentials and the right to pry into the private lives of public figures. Isn't that so?' She was disciplining me but at the same time her voice had no anger or impatience in it.

'I would really appreciate it if you would stop these investigative visits to the neighbourhood. What would you like to know about us?' I sensed a break in her voice as she went on.

'My husband has Alzheimer. And now would you be kind enough to leave.'

I froze as I stood there. I stared at her face, which was full of pain and sadness. Her eyes glistened with tears. I murmured an inaudible apology, turned round and walked away.

A Perfect Relationship

They had reached a stage where they understood each other very well. The discordant note in their relationship had disappeared and Satish appeared very relaxed these days or rather he had been so for many months. Life suddenly assumed a hum drum movement, an idyllic existence, where there were no rough edges. Their relationship had never ever before assumed such calm domesticity.

It had brought to Naina a sense of great relief. She was no longer afraid of being indiscreet with her words that never failed to elicit a strong reprove from Satish. Early on in their marriage she had been very afraid of him. But the recent past had seen some of the best days they had spent together. They agreed on most issues at home. Whether it was a new fridge that had to be bought or she had to make a trip to Jabalpur to see her parents, Satish always agreed most readily. No questions were asked, no mention even of increasing expenses.

There were times when she pondered over this new found bliss. But she never dwelled on it. She was relaxed too. One day as she got ready to go out in the evening, she looked at herself in the mirror as if she was looking at a stranger's image there. She saw a beautiful woman, her hair in a blunt at her shoulders, her brows teasingly arched, her eyes deep and soulful. Her face looked fair and soft and as she smiled at herself, pleased with what she saw, a lovely tantalizing dimple appeared on her right cheek. She was a little taken aback. She was nearly forty-five years old and she was still amazingly attractive to make a man's blood run fast. No wonder she had a few suitors, some of their friends, who made these innocent yet definite passes at her. Champak had playfully pinched her cheek while saying goodbye to her at the gate as she saw him off. Hemant was more direct when he urged her to have dinner with him on an evening when he knew that Satish was not in town. Bhaskar was the importunate suitor who was hurt by her dismissal of him on several occasions. She was tempted to let her blood race, to have some fun but her moorings were secure, her middle class attitudes pretty steadfast.

She loved the new Satish. There was a different tenderness in him that made their lovemaking slow and passionate. She would sleep soundly after that and wake up to the joyful chirping of birds through the windows that lay right behind their bed. She was falling in love anew with her own husband. She felt on top of the world.

'I'd like to visit Madhuri didi this summer'. Her older sister had settled in Geneva, with her husband who was a senior orthopedic surgeon in one of the local hospitals. She had visited her a few years earlier and had enjoyed the walks along the lake, the drives to the end of Lake Geneva, and experienced the slow pace of life in this international city. But it wasn't so simple. Financially they were comfortable but travel abroad was always so expensive.

'Yes. Why not? Let me know your dates and I'll get the tickets done for you. Please take care of the visa application yourself.'

'Both of us should go. You'll be able to escape some part of the summer heat. Madhuri didi will be very pleased if we both visit her.'

'That's not possible. I can't get leave at this stage. I need a period of adjustment with my new boss. I can't ask for leave. It will send the wrong impression.'

She was on cloud nine as she started planning for her trip. Their son Alok had a summer job lined up after his first year at law school. Father and son could bond in summer in her absence. Naina applied for two weeks leave at the firm she worked for and was relieved when her manager agreed.

'Naina, on one condition only. That I get some Swiss chocolates in return.'

She was ecstatic to be able to get away from the long hot Indian summer. Visions of snow peaked mountains, the heavenly green pastures on hillsides, the sleekest bridges spanning valleys, the tranquility of Interlaken, and the warm love of her Madhuri didi encompassing her for two weeks possessed her as she prepared for her vacation. She had a song on her lips, a chirp in her heart as she packed her light woolen clothes for her trip. She must carry the red wrap for those cool evenings in a cafe, sipping coffee in the company of her darling sister, updating her with all news from home.

Soon she had Satish warmed up to her enthusiasm so much so that he took the afternoon off to accompany her to the airport. Naina was touched as it was but a rare gesture on his part. She hugged him tightly as they said goodbye.

'I wish you were coming too,' she said as she moved to join the queue for immigration. He just shook his head. He looked occupied. Maybe he had some important work at office. She will let him go now.

'Satish, you can leave now. You can still manage a few hours of work. It's only three. Thank you. Bye.'

Naina spent the two weeks in Switzerland in a delighted state. Madhuri didi's love and warm hospitality totally de-stressed her. She would wake up in the morning with a feeling of peace in every sinew of her body as if she had no care in the world. The strong full bodied smell of coffee beckoned her in the mornings and the smile on Madhuri didi's face as she entered the kitchen, welcomed the day. Arun Jeejaji was so indulgent in the evenings even after a busy day at the hospital. He would insist on taking them out for dinner for a juicy steak or prepare a delicious salad at home, his contribution to the meal. On weekends the three of them would drive to a nearby resort and take a long walk by the lake before selecting a restaurant for lunch. The alpine flowers, a profusion of primroses, daises and buttercups and the baskets of red geraniums gladdened her heart till every speck of worry disappeared from her body. She felt lighthearted at all times. The green pastures in the countryside with the wonderful fortified castles romanced her soul. The tranquility of Geneva belied its cosmopolitan character.

It was with a very heavy heart that she said goodbye to Madhuri didi and Arun Jeejaji. When they landed she was disappointed to read the brief message from Arun that he was caught up in a meeting and she would have to take a cab home. It was daytime so there was no nervousness on her part. The house looked as if no one had had time to clear up, and this job was now hers to do. Quite mechanically and true to her nature she started putting away things, did two loads of washing in the washing machine, threw some obviously old food lying in the fridge into the trash, changed the sheets till the beds looked inviting. Then she got another message from Arun that he would be held up late for a business meeting followed by dinner.

Alok called to welcome her back and ended the conversation breezily by saying, " Mom, I hope you don't mind. I'm taking Vinita out for dinner and dance at the new disco at the Taj". Vinita was his schoolmate and they got along famously without putting a name to their close relationship. They were always so comfortable with each other, fighting, teasing each other till it made her cry, then making up by taking her out for ice cream, sharing notes, books and whatever it is possible to share between a girl and a boy. Alok was a typical young man, somewhat dominating where women were concerned; Vinita, a delicate, soft spoken girl with an intellectual bent of mind. Naina loved her and at times dreamed of Vinita as a perfect daughter-in-law but she would shrug away the thought. She didn't like disappointments.

Of course, she didn't mind! She was fair enough to think that she had had her fun too. She couldn't grudge her family their routine outings. She made a sandwich for herself, and was fast asleep as soon as her head hit the pillow.

Naina woke up early and as she turned her side she saw Satish sprawled next to her. She moved closer and very tenderly put her arm round his shoulders. He stirred a little but her maternal instinct told her she shouldn't disturb him. So she eased herself out of bed with the minimal movement. Just as she was about to leave for office Alok ran into the kitchen, 'Bye mom. I'm so late!'

'Alok, how was your evening with Vinita? How is she?'

'Tell you all about it in the evening, mom. See you.' And he came over to her, hugged his mother lovingly, something that always disarmed her.

'So, did you and dad enjoy the match? Who won?'

'Oh mom, dad had no time for me. He was never home. I hardly saw him when you were away. Bye, mom, I'm getting late.'

Naina's forehead creased. Father and son had been planning for weeks about the IPL match they were going to watch. There had been endless discussions about the form of the individual players and of course the betting that went with it. Why didn't they go for the match? The tickets were so expensive. She must ask Satish in the evening.

But she never did. For the next two weeks she hardly got time at home. Work had piled up at office. She got home late every evening. Satish too had an important conference to plan for. On the couple of evenings they spent together, Satish seemed unusually preoccupied. One evening as she jabbered on about her vacation, she suddenly paused, looked at Satish and told him in a complaining tone,' You are not even listening to me!'

He turned to her, smiled indulgently and laughed, ' Of course I am, Naina. I'm so glad you enjoyed yourself.'

'Come here,' he patted the couch next to him. She snuggled up to him and the next moment forgot all about her complaint.

A week later they were invited by one of the diplomats posted in India. There was a friendly buzz in the hall as they were ushered in. Men in dinner jackets, suave and stately, and women in their shimmery chiffons and georgettes chatted at their best behaviour. Naina slowly sipped her wine as her eyes scanned the whole room for any acquaintance till her eyes rested on a diva in a bright orange sari speckled with delicate sequins and a red edging that lent it that extra magic. Her face was soft and lovely but the expression very purposeful and businesslike. It was Zarine, the Vice-President of a Pharma company, an Austrian based company that had set up shop in India over a year ago.

Naina was in awe of her. She had met her at parties a few times earlier and she had always felt inadequate as a woman when compared to Zarine. Naina had chided herself for this self flagellation but couldn't help it. Zarine exuded a natural charm and confidence that she was in control of her life. She never seemed to waver, declared what she wanted with complete ease without fumbling for a decision, whether it was to be tea or coffee after dinner. She had the reputation of a hard driving business executive. Her high heeled sophistication combined with a primeval feline grace made her outstanding. She was intimidatingly chic. Her poise and presence at the party unnerved Naina. As she watched her she saw Satish saunter over to her. They seemed to have a conversation that looked private from a distance. Naina noticed that they didn't shake hands. He went over to call a bearer to order a drink for her. Suddenly Naina stood transfixed watching the little tete e tete keenly till her reverie was broken by a voice next to her.

'Keeping an eye on the husband? Enjoy yourself lady, don't break your little heart.' She looked round to face Apparao, a close buddy of Satish, a diplomat of many seasons and storms.

'You look devastating, ma'am.'

Naina always enjoyed his company. Putting people at ease was his forte and he conducted this with great finesse. A bachelor with extravagant habits of intellect and an amateur sportsman of some fame Apparao managed his life as light as a snow flurry. His prowess with the ladies was legendary and he was a very ubiquitous and popular guest at most social events in the city.

'Come, come, let me refill your glass. A party is meant to be enjoyed.' He put his arm protectively round Naina's shoulders and led her towards the middle of the room. Naina moved but her eyes still sought Satish and Zarine. Apparao's guiding arm round her shoulders was not light. It was to shield her from some harm, as if he were leading her away from a scene of accident. Suddenly Naina felt insecure, her step faltered and she leaned against Apparao. The rest of the evening was a blur for her. She had enough wine to feel light headed, danced with a curious abandon with Apparao. Satish was around too but she lost him several times during the evening. She didn't care. She was having a swell time.

The morning dawned and soon she was at her desk. But she couldn't start her work. There was something troubling her. It was an uneasy truth that gnawed at her but she wouldn't face it. Then she confronted it and faced it squarely. Last evening's events unraveled before her eyes bringing with it the clear message that Satish was having an affair with Zarine. It was as clear as the blue sky after a thunderstorm. Naina wondered why she didn't admit it earlier. The calmness of their relationship, the readiness with which Satish permitted her every request, the summer trip to Switzerland. She had been blind.

What should she do? As her world crashed around her, Naina was very calm in her discovery. The confusion in her head cleared and she found new composure. There was enough work to take care of at office and the day went by in feverish activity: meetings, a one on one strategy planning session with her boss and lunch with a client. She needed to be mentally alert and could ill afford the luxury of moping about personal affairs. More self assured, albeit a willed self assurance, made all her tasks suddenly assume a lightness. She was more in control.

Later that evening Naina was fully in command of her emotions, not betraying in any manner the feelings that she had stored in the deep recesses of her psyche. The family had a pleasant dinner, Alok was at his best arguing about the sepulchral presence of septuagenarian and octogenarian politicians in our polity and the need to replace them with bright young people with a modern ethos. It's an uncontested truth dad, he fumed. Naina settled after dinner to watch the news and announced early that she was tired and would like to retire.

The turmoil in her mind did not subside because she didn't confront Satish. Instead, despite the disquietude, she found new energy. Outwardly she displayed no negative emotion, though a discerning eye may have questioned her artificial liveliness and her charged state of mind exhibited itself in a somewhat raised pitch of voice or at other times an unusual softness of tone. She was propelled forward by the spirited words of Scarlet O'Hara, 'Tomorrow is another day'.

Her immediate target was her home. She sought to get rid of the drabness that comes with the same decor over a few years. She disposed off her old furniture, replacing it with new minimalist furniture, giving their living room a new look altogether. New bedspreads, tablecloths, a few new artefacts brought a much needed freshness to her home. The curtain rods were removed, and the curtains replaced with new blinds. The old rug was rolled up and put away. A new solid colour rug brightened the place. She found time to rearrange the wardrobes. A sudden activity of replacing old things, flowers all over, a few green plants in the corner leant the place a charm that was missing all this while. Satish and Alok had raised eyebrows but didn't much care to question this flurry of change, complimenting her on some new acquisition in the evenings.

The preoccupation with redecorating her home and office took care of her waking hours where she never allowed herself to indulge in any recriminations. The nights were a little difficult and there was no physical relationship left. Naina was aloof but normal otherwise and Satish obviously didn't miss it. That hurt her but she overcame it with her will power and steely nerves. A few months went by.

It was a cool winter morning on a Sunday and Naina had settled down in an easy chair with a cup of tea and the newspaper. Outside it was still grey and the morning sun had not broken through the overnight misty atmosphere. The sips of hot tea suffused her with a warmth and unknown peace. She decided she would let the day pan out without making any effort to do anything in particular. She skimmed through the newspaper. Suddenly a tremor passed through her body when she read that Zarine would shortly be joining as the new chief of South Asia for her company in Singapore. Naina got up, made herself another cup of tea and snuggled back into the chair with a throw over her legs.

She heard Satish walk into the lounge. She looked up, gave him a beaming, welcome smile, 'Good morning'.

'Good morning. You look very comfortable'. And he bent down to give her a peck on the cheek.

'It's a beautiful day. How about taking my wife out for lunch at The Terrace?'

'I'd love that Satish. Would you like a cup of tea?' Naina smiled to herself as she walked into the kitchen.

The Courtyard

Taiji was always seated on a string cot in the corner of the courtyard. From that vantage point she not only conducted her daily activities but also surveyed the whole courtyard and the rooms that opened out on it. Her day was spent in cutting vegetables for meals, cleaning the dal in a thali before it went into the kitchen for cooking. She constantly gave instructions to the maid who came for a couple of hours in the morning to do the cleaning and any other odd jobs she was assigned. Ma would often solicit her help and assistance with food being prepared for the family. Taiji would prepare the spices for making pickles, she would put out the red chilies for drying and she would spread the ground dal mixed with spices into small uneven balls for sun drying which are later stored for the year for curries. These annual culinary rituals were her forte which were indispensable for the family's needs.

Taiji had been with them as long as Rasna could remember. She had been widowed at a young age, remarriage was unthinkable but the kindness accorded to her in her marital home saw her through long years with respect and security. When Rasna was a young girl Taiji would braid her hair into two neat plaits for school. It was always Taiji who would give her a glass of milk in the morning while Ma would prepare her tiffin for school, two small paranthas with pickle. Rasna enjoyed the flavours of the spicy and sour pickles. Her choice of pickles for school became more eclectic as she grew older, the humble mango pickle giving way to the more refined adult flavours of ginger, lemon, jackfruit and whole red chilly pickle. Every time Taiji made a new pickle she would very lovingly urge Rasna to try it, explaining the exotic flavours and the particular spice that enhanced its taste. Rasna's favourites were of course the sweet mango preserves, and the plum chutney that Taiji prepared diligently and with affection for the family and which were the delicious accompaniments to their simple vegetarian food.

When Rasna returned from school Taiji always welcomed her with some ripe, succulent fruit, a guava, or the sweetest of mangoes, or it would be a bowl of mulberries or grapes. Rasna's favourite was ripe but still fresh tamarind, as if it had ripened on the tree and had just been plucked. Rasna loved the delicious taste of tamarind. She would sit on the cot with Taiji, enjoy the fruit and share with her the day's events at school. For Taiji also it was a pleasurable break in her day and the two would either talk conspiratorially or laugh loudly over some school anecdote that Rasna related to her embellished with exaggerations that the two enjoyed.

Now Rasna was in second year of college, her two plaits had given way to a single plait. She had tried to change her hair style, very conservatively, by getting it trimmed up to her waist and leaving it open. And, oh my god, what shock waves had gone through the household as her father hollered at her mother in their room. Ma had borne the full impact of his wrath as his anger spilled on to her. Ma did not speak a word as she waited for his fury to dissipate.

'I will not tolerate my daughter walking on the road with her hair open. It is your responsibility to teach her how to conduct herself. Can't you keep an eye on your daughter? Shame on you!'

It was her father's writ that ran at home. Patriarchal authoritarianism at its worst. The family members dare not challenge it. Their submission to their father's diktats was total. When he was at home all was quiet and peaceful and everyone went about doing whatever had to be done without a sound. They heaved a sigh of relief when he left for his shop. The day was spent in relaxation. Ma went about her work with a song on her lip. Theirs was a disciplined family. Rasna and her brother whom everybody addressed as Veerji were very close to their mother. She saw to all their comforts and indulged their every request.

Dulari was a pleasant woman, brought up in a happy joint family of numerous aunts and cousins. She would not question her husband's authority and had submitted to it but retained her sense of humour and her cheerfulness. There were times when the earth around her shook as her husband's anger made her shudder inwardly but she withstood these onslaughts as but petty disturbances in her life. She was made of sterner stuff. Her mantra in life was to have a happy household that reverberated with the tinkling of laughter and music. She doted on her two children, her lovely daughter and her son who she knew would always protect his mother. She loved pretty clothes and like a beautiful angel traversing the house all day, her anklets musical, her invariably matching bangles clinking as she went about her duties. The summer dorias and the organdies and organzas gave way to cascading georgettes and crepes and heavy silks as winter approached. She was popular in the neighbourhood and the women would very often walk in to chat over a cup of tea.

Dulari often thought about Champa, her daily help who came in the morning and managed all the needling chores in her home. The lives of the ordinary poor Indian women are so uncertain, full of stress, anger, shortages, deprivation, difficult relationships. There's no rationality about it. Is the husband's job secure? Will the landlord throw them out next month if they're unable to pay rent? Will her sick child survive the winter? Will her daughter be happy in her new home? Will her husband be kind to her? Will her mother-in-law harass her or will she love her? She wondered how they managed their lives. The lives of the poor are always in the hands of the gods they pray to. This kind of uncertainty would kill her. And yet they're so cool. Champa was like that. She looked well fed, was certainly not the emaciated, undernourished, thin women wrapped in saris that she saw on the streets. And she was a lively one, smiling and joking with Taiji and Dulari all the time. Very often she would ask Rasna to let her oil her beautiful hair. But Rasna hated the touch of oil to her head. Champa always came in smiling and was ever so pleased if Dulari gave her something special to eat or an old sari that would be added to her meagre wardrobe.

It was a good life until the day Rasna returned home drenched to the skin and late in the evening. Dulari had been beside herself with fear, dreading that her husband would return home to find Rasna missing. Dulari opened the door and there stood Rasna like an apparition, her clothes soaking wet, her hair plastered to her head and beads of water twinkling on her face. And a look that was apologetic, yet defiant.

'What happened to you? Where have you been? Why didn't you call?' The barrage of questions went unanswered as Rasna stepped into the door and made an effort to go to her room. But Dulari caught her wrist and held her back.

'I asked you something. Where were you all this time? Why have you been walking in the rain? Answer me.'

'Ma, please let me change. I'm feeling cold.'

'Of course you'll be cold. Where did you go after college? Why didn't you take an autorickshaw? How did you get wet?'

There had been a thunderstorm in the late afternoon with the winds so strong they threatened to bring down all the trees in the neighbourhood. And the rain came down in sheets, not letting up for two hours. The courtyard was full of water up to the ankles. The guava tree in the corner was everybody's favourite and it looked as if it would give way to the elements. Only when the rain stopped did the water finally drain away. Dulari's mind was not peaceful as she waited for Rasna to return home.

Rasna broke free and ran to her room at the far end of the courtyard and locked herself in. Heaving a sigh of relief that her father hadn't returned home, Rasna was confident she could handle her mother. It had been touch and go. She quickly changed into a warm dry suit, undid her plait, gave her hair a shake with the towel under the fan and combed it furiously till it looked somewhat dry. She was still shivering but her hair must be dry before her father returned so she couldn't put the fan off. Under no circumstances did she want her wet hair to give her away.

She shuddered at the thought of being confronted with her father's wrath. She had been twelve years old at the time. It was the age of bloom for young girls and the best pleasures of life were spending time with your best friend. At the time their neighbours were the Bansals. Their daughter Aditi was the same age as Rasna and the two girls were soul mates, going to the same school, spending hours after school together, huddled in each others company. That day Aditi was going to see a movie with her family and urged Rasna to come with them. It was a Sunday and Rasna ran home to get permission. Her parents were in their room, her father was lying on the bed and Ma was pressing his feet.

'Aditi is going to see a film with her family. I want to go with them.' And the words were out before she realized she had made a mistake.

'Now, it is you who decides what you want to do.' Her father's tone was ominous.

Rasna was in a defiant mood. She so wanted to go.

'Yes, can I go please? Let me go please.'

'There's no need to see a film. Young girls your age have no business seeing films.'

'But all my friends go. I want to go.'

Rasna's rebellious tone was enough to exacerbate the situation. Her father refused, she broke into tears at the same time insisting she wanted to go. Her pleading and stubbornness made him angrier till he was screaming at her.

'Don't you dare speak like that. And your punishment is, ask forgiveness for your behaviour by rubbing you nose to the ground and say you'll never speak like that again. Rub your nose to the ground!'

Dulari made a movement as if to suggest that was unthinkable but she was silenced too.

'I said rub your nose to the ground and say sorry!'

Rasna's tears streamed down her cheeks. She mumbled an apology but her father insisted. She trembled with humiliation, she looked at her mother for some support which was not forthcoming. Ultimately she went down on her knees, did as she was told and in utter shame collapsed on the floor into a heap hugging her knees. She had no energy to get up and face anybody.

All bonds between a father and daughter were snapped that day. Rasna felt such humiliation that she was unable to eat for a week, she became weak, had a fever and missed school too. Taiji and Dulari were speechless with muted horror that Rasna, their darling girl had been treated so abjectly and no one spoke to one another in the family for days. Their concern was Rasna whom they finally nursed back to health. She was young but the indelible shame of that day scarred her inner being and her consciousness. She came closer to her mother and Taiji and did not speak to her father for years. It was her unspoken and undemonstrated hostility towards her father, palpable, yet dared not be conveyed in any manner. But it simmered within her. However, in that moment a defiance, a revolt was born. With the passing years Rasna hardly ever thought about it. It lay dormant within her. Today as she was reminded of it a shiver ran down her spine and with good cause and she was on her guard.

When she emerged from her room, she saw that Taiji was sitting in the verandah. In the aftermath of the thunderstorm the verandah was cool and Rasna sat down next to Taiji and watched the reflection of the light on the wet verandah very thoughtfully. Taiji gave Rasna a long enquiring look. Rasna said nothing. The evening passed without an event.

Rasna was safe. She ate her dinner in silence and avoided any proximity to Taiji or Ma.

The next morning as Rasna emerged from her room Taiji called out to her. She was dressed in a crisp light blue sari that accentuated her fair skin, crisscrossed with very fine wrinkles on the face and forearms.

'Rasna, come here. Where were you last night?'

'I'm getting late for college. We have an early class.'

'Today is Wednesday. You never go early on Wednesdays.' Taiji sounded annoyed and skeptical.

Not wanting to raise any heckles Rasna laughed, 'Of course Taiji. But I've opted for some extra tutorials.'

'Rasna, come here. I want to see your new suit. You look lovely! What pretty silver jhumkas! Why are you wearing these to college?' And she began a monologue on how utterly spoilt girls were nowadays. Rasna could however detect an under current in Taiji's words. She didn't care. She'll ask her later. Right now, she must run.

The following weeks Taiji watched Rasna keenly. There was a not too subtle a transformation taking place in this young woman. Her face had a new healthy colour, her pink hued cheeks and her bright dancing eyes lent an ethereal charm. She looked happy conceding a smile ever so often. She always appeared in full control of herself, confident, with a serious preoccupation at the same time. There was a certain gravitas about her too. The playful girlishness was gone. She still bantered with Taiji and Dulari but the purposefulness in her demeanour was not entirely lost on the two women. They were perplexed and delighted at the same time. She had begun to help at home, take care of a number of tasks. Rasna would insist on making the evening tea for Dulari and Taiji. They would watch her reading late into the night and find her books open at her desk in the morning, sheaves of notes lying about. Dulari could now entrust her with buying random groceries.

'Rasna, please don't be late today. Nidhi bua is coming in the afternoon".

'Rasna, how could you forget to pick up my blouses from the tailor?'

'Rasna, did you pick up the hair oil?'

'Rasna, Rasna, Rasna, how could you be late today? I needed your help with dinner for your father's friends.'

The day dawned with a distinct nip in the air. Dulari shivered as she stepped into the courtyard in the morning. Taiji had a shawl wrapped around her shoulders and was sipping warm tea with obvious pleasure. The grey sky made the chill even more menacing. Dulari thought she must prepare some hot breakfast for the family, a warm upma with some carrots, cauliflower and peas with a dollop of ghee to make it nourishing. She could hear some sounds emanating from Rasna's room along with soft music. Giving up the idea of calling out to

Rasna she quickened her step towards the kitchen. A little later Rasna surprised her with a tight hug from the back.

'What are you preparing Ma? Oh! upma. Good. Please pack me some for college today. And could you also pack some paranthas for me Ma? I have a tutorial today. Feel like having your paranthas with pickle today. Please.'

'Ok, ok, Rasna. Let me get your fathers breakfast ready first. Then I'll make the paranthas.'

'Thanks Ma. My beautiful Ma.' And Rasna gave Dulari another tight hug, her head lingering at her shoulder an imperceptible moment longer. Dulari loved this show of affection from her daughter and smiled as she patted Rasna's cheek.

Today Rasna did not seem to be in a hurry to rush to college. She lingered over breakfast with her mother and Taiji. When she left she had a bag slung over her shoulder, a pretty jhola, embroidered in red and yellow that Dulari had bought for her from an exhibition. She had been carrying her books in that bag now for a few weeks.

'Rasna, your bag looks heavy today.'

'Ma, Mandira wants to borrow some books from me.'

Rasna gave Taiji a hug.

'I may be a little late today. Don't bother making a snack in the evening Taiji.'

'And Ma, I've made my bed and put away my things. Just tell Champa to sweep my room. Bye.'

And she was gone.

As the evening wore on and the darkness became deeper Dulari was overtaken by a sudden fear. Rasna hadn't returned home. It was time for her father to return home from work. She opened the main door several times and looked down the street, her eyes piercing the darkness for her daughter. She went into Rasna's room. The room looked neat, her desk was cleared of all books and papers. She opened her wardrobe and almost shuddered at the sight. There were just two old salwar suits in it. It was almost empty. She looked around the room in a frenzy. And then she saw the white envelope under the lamp on the writing table. The sound of the front door opening and her husbands voice filled her with dread.

Dulari walked into the courtyard and without a word handed the white envelope to her husband.

The House on Nawab Yusuf Road

The old bungalow had two high wrought iron gates. The drives on either side of the bungalow led to the two side entrances of the bungalow if you went straight down those drives. However, the drive on either side also curved, leading to the porch at the centre of the bungalow. The landlord himself lived in the front part of the house with access through the porch. There was a large garden in front beyond the porch. The lawn was inelegantly bordered by flower beds and beyond that a hedge that ran all along the drives from the porch to the two gates. There were a few shrubs in the garden, red hibiscus, champa, yellow lantana that lent it some colour.

If you drove straight from the gates instead of going towards the porch you reached the side entrances to the two portions of the house occupied by the two tenants. There were three rooms in each unit which lay towards the back of the house. There was a verandah that ran the entire width of the house at the back with a spacious courtyard beyond. Both the verandah and the courtyard had been divided into two by a seven-foot wall that ran through the middle. The barrack like structure at the end of the wall was where the two kitchens of the tenants were located. This was probably the original kitchen of yore of the colonial bungalow, located a good twenty-five to thirty feet away from the main building. And the only communication between the two neighbours was the little wicket gate at the end of the wall.

We occupied the right apartment within the bungalow if you can call it that. The other portion had been lying vacant for a few months and Sudha, the landlord's wife complained that they were losing rent every month. And then one day I heard sounds on the other side of the verandah, sounds of stuff being carried to the kitchen beyond. I was glad I was going to have a neighbour at last.

I met Malini a few days later. The entrances to our homes were on opposite sides of the big bungalow, the only hope of a chance meeting lay in an encounter across the wicket gate at the end of the dividing wall. The gate was low and had a sliding bolt on each side, locked with a padlock by both occupants to preserve their privacy and security. A week or so after they moved in, I spotted her on my way to the kitchen and greeted her. She gave a shy, wan smile but her greeting was welcoming, and it encouraged me. She immediately conveyed the warm impression that she was pleased to see me. She was a beautiful woman, fair of face, a full but slim body. Her hair went down her back in a thick plait. The dark blue sari she was wearing accentuated the paleness and the colour on her face.

It was midday, the children were at school, and I readily agreed when she invited me in for a cup of tea. I learnt that she had two boys, aged seven and five. Her husband, she said, had come to the city as the manager of a popular restaurant there. From our first meeting started a friendship that was unusual in that it needed no years of acquaintance or togetherness. It was as if we had known each other forever. Her husband, Mohan worked late at the restaurant. My husband was also a workaholic and kept long hours at the office. The result was that Malini and I spent our days together, going shopping for our groceries together in the mornings, or chatting over cups of tea in the forenoons. The children fed after school would run away to play in the neighbourhood and once again we would sit together in the early evenings to cut vegetables for the evening meal till such time as the kids' homework had to be supervised or Prashant returned from office. The locks on the wicket gate were opened first thing in the morning and locked just prior to going to bed.

The pre monsoon air was heavy with clouds and the sultry day was very oppressive and one could scarcely breathe. As I walked listlessly towards the kitchen, I noticed that Malini had not opened the lock on the wicket gate. My brow somewhat puzzled I went about my morning work like an automaton. I could hear no sounds too on the other side of the wall. Around noon I went around to their side of the bungalow to talk to Malini.

She appeared at the door and I immediately sensed something was wrong. Her eyes gave away nothing, but she looked very serious. Without being invited in, I stepped into the room and noticed Mohan was there.

'Oh, you haven't gone to work as yet'.

Sensing some tension in the air, I said, 'Oh, I'm sorry to disturb you'.

And as I walked out, I noticed a man sitting on a chair to my left. Nobody made any attempt at introductions, so I beat a hasty retreat thoroughly perplexed. They had a guest and were obviously busy.

The rain came down in torrents that evening, and it continued to rain throughout the night. The bungalow was old, with a high roof built for making the indoors cool through summer. But the roof was tiled with indigenous tiles that invariably developed a leak when it rained. I had to place buckets and kitchen vessels here and there where the roof leaked. The schools were about to reopen after the summer vacations and Malini and I had to make a couple of trips to the market to get school supplies for the children. But for three days there was no sign of her and I hesitated going again to the other side.

On the fourth day I spotted her through the wicket gate and enquired quite innocently,

'Are you still busy with your guest?'

'Yes. No, he has left but I have some work.'

Her ambivalent reply again puzzled me but out of respect for her I did not pursue with my questions. She looked thoughtful and her countenance was serious enough for me to restrain myself.

As the days passed without any communication from Malini I was very bewildered. We had become such good friends, held back nothing from each other and in fact our lives were simple transparent lives. Why had she stopped communicating with me? I did not know who their visitor was. Why did she not tell me? Questions such as these floated in my mind all day. I broached the subject with Prashant only to be chided for unnecessary intrusion into others' lives.

The chink in the wall that allowed me a peep into her life had been shut. It was like hedges that guard the privacy of the residents solidly permitting outsiders only a very small keyhole view of the inside. As a passerby longs to get a peek into the secret life behind the hedge, I too desired an explanation for Malini's behaviour. But I was left guessing, much to my discomfort.

Three days later Malini suddenly appeared at the door. 'The kids have gone to school. Let's go and get their books and exercise books.' A matter of fact statement made in a matter of fact manner. The unusual passage of the preceding days was not a subject for discussion. It was mutually and silently agreed. We resumed our lives from where we had left off and soon it was as if there had been no interregnum. Once again, we spent all our spare time together and respected the unspoken pact between us.

The monsoon season was over. The days began to become cooler. The festival season was around the corner. Malini and I fasted the eight days of Navratri with full rituals. We would have our evening meal together all the days of fasting. The day prior to Dusherra Malini and I took the children to the penultimate day of Ramlila.

The next day dawned as usual and I thought I should decide with Malini the time for the evening extravaganza of Dusshera. The wicket gate was locked. We've all overslept today, I thought to myself. I got busy with household work. When I remembered I sent my older one to find out from Malini what time we should leave for Ramlila grounds. He came back saying that the wicket gate was still locked. Something stirred inside me. There was no sound from the other side of the wall.

Dusshera day passed, a week went by and still no sign of Malini. Even Prashant noticed the unusual situation, but he was back at work with renewed energy after the holiday season. My earlier perplexity now turned into a kind of resentment at such behaviour. How could she take me for granted like this, locking me out whenever she wanted to? I was simmering with self justified irritation at such inexplicable conduct.

The weather had become very cool and I sat in the verandah, enjoying the solitude and peace when I heard the sound of the wicket gate being opened. Here she comes, I thought angrily, without any explanation to offer for her absence all these days. Malini came up to the verandah and just stood there before me. I looked up at her reproachfully, ready to say a few unkind words and demand an explanation for her absence all these days. But one look at her face and I jumped up and hugged her and asked kindly,

'What happened, Malini?' She looked terrible. Her beautiful eyes were red as if she had been crying for a long time. There was intense pain in her expression. Her sari was worn without any care. I was full of concern.

'Malini, what's wrong? Come, sit here. Can I get you a cup of tea?' She nodded without speaking. I left her and ran into the kitchen to make tea for her.

When I came back with the tea, she looked calmer as if she had now left her fate in my hands. Handing her the cup of tea I said,

'Now, tell me what is it that is bothering you?'

She sipped her tea slowly, looked up at me, hesitated, and with an expression of trepidation said,

'Promise me that you will not tell anyone what I am going to tell you today. Not even Prashant. Promise me'

'Malini, what is bothering you? Of course, I won't tell anyone.'

'Jaya, how to tell you what I have been going through. My life has turned topsy-turvy.'

I wasn't prepared for the narrative that left her lips for the next two hours. The day progressed. I became cold as I sat spellbound listening to Malini. She poured out her heart, without holding back anything. There was utter despair in her words as she confided in me her life's story with all its tribulations, fears, uncertainties for the future. I was dumbfounded. Her story was unbelievable as she blurted it out. At times she spoke calmly, at other times in deep anguish.

'I got married about ten years ago, but not to Mohan. Balraj was in the Himachal Pradesh civil service and posted at Palanpur. Immediately after the wedding he took me to Palanpur with him. He was a very kind man and took good care of me and showed a lot of love and affection for me. We had a small house in Palanpur. It was a quiet, very beautiful place with the majestic hills all around us. When he returned from office in the evenings, we would go for long walks together along the gorge, with the hills surrounding us.

One day as we walked in the bazaar, Balraj met an old childhood friend and he was very pleased to see him. They hugged and backslapped endlessly. I stood on watching them till his friend asked him,

'Won't you introduce me?'

'Of course, Mohan. This is my wife, Malini.'

The two had parted company after college. Balraj had joined the state civil service whereas Mohan went away to work in Bombay.

'From that day onwards, Mohan spent a lot of time with us. He was a manager at the local club. He became a regular visitor at our home. His weekly holiday would be spent mostly with us. Balraj and Mohan would reminisce about their childhood, over endless cups of tea and pakoras. We would relish the good food I cooked for them in each others company. The three of us would go to see films at the local theatre. Mohan and I had a relationship that was comfortable, cordial and friendly. We were both much younger than Balraj. He had married late and my family never had any qualms about marrying me off to a man twelve years my senior in age. Mohan teased me constantly about my gullibility and innocence insisting that I needed to question the world around me. There was never a hint of jealousy or disapproval of our relationship where Balraj was concerned.

'Soon there was a change of jobs for Balraj. His new job involved a lot of touring in the state. When he first started to go out on tour for a day or two, he would request Mohan to take care of me. Mohan usually came in the evening and as usual I would cook a simple meal and share it with him. These evenings spent with Mohan with Balraj away became a regular feature in my life. We would discuss movies, the music, Nargis and Raj Kapoor. We would exchange the novels of Prem Chand and Sharat Chandra. Those innocent evenings spent in Mohan's company were some of the best days of my life.

Mohan and I became very good friends and as Balraj's work took him away from home quite frequently we spent a lot of time together.

A couple of years went by. My relationship with Balraj was more that of a friend than a lover.'

I looked incredulously and sympathetically at Malini. She went on without hesitating, the floodgates of her story having finally opened unabashedly.

'Balraj wanted a child but was unable to as our relationship had never been consummated. His frustration was palpable in bed though I must admit that I was not so perturbed as a woman. I came to know later that he had confided in Mohan about his inability to satisfy me or himself. I began to notice a change in Mohan's behaviour towards me that was certainly not imperceptive. There was a distinct change in his look, the way he approached me. Balraj began to leave us alone together more than ever. He was required to go to Haridwar for the Kumbh preparations for three days. We had dinner together the previous night and he mentioned his trip very casually and then told Mohan to keep an eye on me.'

'Mohan's tentative overtures now became explicit yet tender and I began to respond to him. The first day he took me out for a film followed by a chana bhatura dinner. In the cinema hall his hand first rested on my arm and then he held my hand. It was a startling new sensation for me, and my youthful body gave in very easily.'

'After a few weeks only I conceived. I broke the news to Balraj in a most matter of fact manner. Balraj was

65

overjoyed yet he maintained an outward silence. He would allow us to spend time together. Mohan would come in when Balraj left for office. The baby was born in winter, the cold enveloping me and my baby. There was confusion in our lives, one that could not be resolved. I loved my little son and wanted to share him with both Mohan and Balraj.'

'Here are the pictures of his first birthday. Then our second son was born. Balraj began to withdraw into himself. He was a distant father in every respect. As time went by, I feared for my boys and their future. I tried to make up for the absence of a real, devoted and committed father for them. I spoke to Mohan about it, pleaded with him that he could not ignore his responsibilities. He was prepared to take care of the boys provided I married him. They needed a father, and one who was interested in their welfare. He was their biological father after all.'

'And then my opportunity came when Mohan was offered a job here and I toyed with the idea of a move with him. I simply left a note for Balraj and left. There was no time to think or ponder. This was the natural consequence of our peculiar lives. I never looked back for a moment. We had to do it for the sake of our boys. However, there were distressing moments when I thought of Balraj and I was filled with a sense of guilt and treachery. He had given me a new life with Mohan, and I had deserted him. But my new life here was a blessing which I wished to savour for the sake of each one of us.'

'Three months passed. We didn't hear from Balraj. And then he came the day you saw him.'

And I remembered the thoughtful looking gentleman sitting in a corner of the room when I had barged into Malini's home.

'He was very pained by our decision to leave without informing him. He understood the inevitability of this relationship and realized that it had become an untenable situation. It could not be sustained any more, but he still asserted his right over his wife. I was after all his lawfully wedded wife and could not desert him in this manner. Yet he acknowledged the utter hopelessness of our continuing relationship. He is a good man, Jaya. He never blamed Mohan for it knowing fully well that he had thrown us together. All three of us were quite devastated by our circumstances.

And yet there was only one solution. But nobody had the courage to speak candidly about it. We all hesitated. He stayed for three days and left. I was shaken to the core. My life was once again at the crossroads. There was but one route I could take but didn't know how to do it. He came again as you know. Mohan spoke to him but not in my presence. Balraj was very fond of me and didn't wish to let go of me. He felt that we could all live together as we had done for years. He refused to confront the reality that the boys were growing up and would be faced with a peculiar predicament-- whose name would they adopt? At the same time Mohan and I did not wish to hurt him in any way.

We are where we left off when he left yesterday. I don't know what to do Jaya.'

Malini had a very troubled look on her face. I was stunned by her story. It was time for the children to return home from school so we parted company on that uncertain note. I was helpless and unable to suggest anything. Our lives went on in the same humdrum manner but there had crept into it a seriousness that was unavoidable. The innocence of Malini and my friendship with her was wrought with the pain of her story. I must now too carry that burden. It could not be brushed aside even though I steered clear of any mention of it in our day to day activities.

The cool days of winter were giving way to a new welcome warmth in the atmosphere. Homes, gardens, traffic roundabouts were awash with a riot of colour. The poppies, the pansies, the dianthus, the phlox and the antirrhinum filled our lives with joy and colour. The dahlias were magnificent, majestic round faces reminding us of the beauty of nature. Housewives took pride in their gardens and communities organized best garden contests for the residents.

The windy days of march brought more sunshine and dust blew all over with the wind. It was time for a change in the households and we were all busy putting away the quilts and blankets and our woolen clothes. The children were busy with their annual examinations and constantly looked forward to when these would be over, and they would all be free to play all day. Malini and I planned the summer days ahead planning summer activities to keep the children busy.

I was just settling down to enjoy a little rest in the hot afternoon when Malini rushed in and said,

'Jaya, Balraj has had a heart attack. He wants all of us to come immediately.'

I helped her pack and prepared some food for them for the journey. They left by the night train.

I didn't hear from her for over two weeks. Mohan came back after ten days but Malini stayed on to take care of Balraj. This present arrangement was totally unacceptable to Mohan, but he had no moral authority to assert himself. He had to swallow the bitter pill. He had my confidence and was quite relieved to be able to speak frankly with me about the sudden turn his life had taken once more. What was it that compelled Malini to be responsible for Balraj? He desired her unqualified loyalty towards him now. Mohan could not understand her compulsion in her relationship with Balraj. They were both torn between their consideration for Balraj and their now stable love for each other.

The summer heat grew intense. It was on a hot June afternoon that Mohan came to inform me that Balraj passed away of cardiac arrest. He left and came back with Malini after ten days. The first tempestuous shower with all its fury came down on the parched earth as the three of us stood in the local temple to solemnize the wedding vows of Malini and Mohan. I was thrilled as they garlanded each other, and the priest blessed them.

The Ashram

Sujata sat under the tamarind tree quietly and looked around her. It was a tranquil summer afternoon; the heat had dissipated the energy of all around her but she sat peacefully under the cool shade of the tamarind tree. The morning's work had been completed, the girls and boys had retired into their huts. Murli and Pushpa liked their well-earned rest at this time of the day. Only the gardener, Todarmal, had been pottering around and could not be seen now. Sujata shut her eyes and a waxy slumber seemed to overtake her. And then she heard footsteps. She opened her eyes and saw Todarmal standing a few meters away.

'Someone has come to meet you,' he said.

And before she could enquire she saw someone twenty meters away, walking towards her. A few muscles in her body became instantly taut but she straightened her back and let her facial muscles relax intentionally in order to assume a normal, formal countenance.

'What are you saying? Your disapproval kills the soul of another. It makes the other person seem worthless in their own eyes. You can kill someone's self confidence. I am going away. And please do not ask me where I'm going. In good time I'll let you know where I am but not now.'

After five years she had written to him, a very polite letter telling him where she was and a few sentences about what she was doing. He had replied in very warm words how he appreciated what she was doing and asked her if she would like some financial assistance for the ashram. She had not replied.

Today they were face to face after six years. He still looked very handsome and dapper but the greyness and the older look made him even more distinguished and desirable than ever. The sartorial change of white khadi kurta and pyjama really became him. His lean and fit physique betrayed the disciplined daily workout. She felt her blood race not with desire but with a nervousness and fear of herself and him. She loved her present and frugal life and had forsaken her earlier life. Life had taken on a new meaning.

Her hostess introduced them and said, 'Nina is a lawyer.'

'Are you a practising lawyer? Where do you practice?' Sujata asked.

'Well, I have a law degree but I'm not a practicing lawyer. I advise my friends when they need some legal advice and my knowledge of law comes in very handy in property disputes. You know, pro bono work. I've had to deal with my brothers over our mother's property and they know they can't fool me because I'm a lawyer.'

And then she went on to regale them with an animated account of her mother's will, how she had left a will saying that she, her daughter, would have an equal share in her property. Oh, these decadent descendants of hot priceless property that their parents had acquired decades ago but now was a lucrative source of income for the next generation! It was disgusting to hear them gush about where they lived and right now this woman lawyer and her brothers were driving her crazy.

'My younger brother said he didn't want to live in Vasant Vihar. His only choice was West End.'

And she went on, mindlessly imagining the listeners had any interest in her. Sujata stood up abruptly and walked across to where her gracious hostess, Bela, a gentle woman, was talking to the erstwhile minister for Civil Aviation. Not wanting to deny Bela her tete e tete with her honuorable guest, she decided not to approach them even though he was one minister she enjoyed talking to when they met at parties. He was pleasant and approachable and interested in you. Some of these younger icons of authority had still not acquired the vague, distant look of a stranger that the older, insufferable ones always sported, their scaly look very difficult to penetrate or understand. She must make a quiet exit; nobody will notice her absence.

She motioned to him to sit down. They sat in silence for a while, with a calmness surrounding them that had never existed earlier.

'I don't feel well. I'll stay at home.' Her head was splitting with migraine.

'You just need an excuse not to go. You know very well this is important for me. The ambassador and the commerce minister of state will be there. Can't you smile and make polite talk and be like the other women! What a useless wife you are!'

'I can't, Bharat. All those fashionable women loaded in diamonds talking of helping the poor, fawning over people in high places. It's all such a sham!'

They had been invited to cocktails by the Kapurs, to welcome the new Japanese ambassador. Ghazala was Andy Kapur's wife. She was certainly not a stunning beauty but her lavish style made her stand out. Well coiffured hair, bright sequined clothes, tantalizing necklines, glittering solitaires, a piquant expression, high heels, all defined her as one of the most fashionable women in the city. And the smile, wide smiles that escaped her face, lured those around her till she was the cynosure of all eyes. She could ensnare anyone as she flitted around parties. Sujata admired her energy but she couldn't replicate it. Her quiet demeanour was her undoing as she recoiled from Bharat's verbal assault after every party. Their nights would be ruined, he would storm out of the bedroom.

The ashram had been her haven since she left home. She had met Professor Aruna Kashyap at the book launch of a retired bureaucrat. Professor Kashyap normally led a reclusive life at the ashram but she was in Delhi for some medical consultation and Sujata's cousin, the esteemed author, had persuaded Professor Kashyap to come for the book launch. Surprisingly, Professor Kashyap had agreed quite willingly to speak on the occasion, commending the author on his account of the remote tribal areas and the peculiar and explosive problems they now encountered. Her own sociological background made her understanding acute to the point where she urged the small gathering to action and exhorted the power of the academics to play a more active role. It was a deviation from her usual non-interfering stance but then the rajdhani always propelled people to action. Sujata had gone to the book launch with an old classmate from college and sat thoughtful and pensive after listening to Aruna.

But today they sat under the cool shade of the tamarind tree, neither with any expectation of the other. Sujata liked his calm presence, she wanted to lean against his shoulder, or nestle in his arms, she wished he would hold her face tenderly in his hands and kiss her cheeks lightly. She would simply surrender to his embrace. Then the realization hit her. She had been missing him painfully all these years, but no, she would never admit it to herself. They had always enjoyed a togetherness despite their contrasting temperaments and that was the deep love they shared for each other. Sujata was blessed with a calm temperament that was her strength whereas Bharat was intense, capable, very pragmatic but madly in love with his wife and she knew it.

It had been an instant attraction, albeit at first fairly physical as both were extremely good looking. Sujata was tall, of a dusky fair complexion, a full body that no man could resist, beautiful black eyes, long black hair and a gait that was so sensuous that men would be mesmerized when she walked into a room. Bharat was the spoilt successor of a business empire that his grandfather had built. But his sharp intellect, honed by a Harvard education did not make a dandy out of him. On the contrary business was infused with a new energy that Bharat's youthfulness contributed to it.

They had met at the Jaipur Literature Festival. Sujata was working for a publishing house at the time.

'You'll enjoy the candidness of this autobiography. I liked the intellectual honesty of the author.' Sujata said to the young man who had handed her the book to pay for it. It was normally not her wont to chat with strangers but this one was too handsome to be ignored. Did he just walk off the ramp? His day old unshaven face quite complimented his conservative blue blazer and grey worsted trousers. He was tall, with a lean David physique and Sujata was embarrassed by her gaze that had rested on him moments longer than necessary while he was paying for his book.

'I think I'll enjoy a cup of coffee with the beautiful lady to begin with.' Taken aback at the offer from a total stranger she was even more shocked by her response. Sujata had been standing in for a friend at the till in the bookshop that was doing brisk business at the festival.

'Sure. I'll join you outside in five minutes.'

The aroma of the coffee had a bewitching effect on them both as they sat and chatted, oblivious of the crowds milling around them. Bharat took her out to dinner at the hotel where he was staying. It was a tempestuous affair after that and six months later they were married. Theirs was a gentle yet a torrid relationship.

Never attracted towards any other woman his one love was Sujata. They had no kids but he didn't care. He even respected her need to live her life on her own terms but he missed her sorely. He wanted her back in his life. The years without Sujata had been lonely.

'Come back home Sujata. I miss you. You've been away too long. No more please.'

Sujata did not reply but her heart wrenched and she was rattled by his presence.

'Let's take a walk round the ashram Bharat.'

As they strolled through the grounds of the ashram Bharat was conscious of a pervading peace and serenity that touched him deeply. It was afternoon, there was no one to be seen, a slumber enveloped the atmosphere. Even the brilliant yellow blooms of the amaltas, hanging in long bunches were drooping like the eyes of a weary traveler. The mango and the tamarind trees exuded a coolness under which he and Sujata walked as if for time immemorial. The occasional splash of colour of the gulmohar was reminiscent of the passion they found in each other that lit up their lives. Only the rustle of leaves under their feet were a reminder of human presence in nature. Bharat felt he belonged to this grove and this woman. The three were inseparable, the beautiful woman beside him, the magnificent trees, and he were part of one whole in creation.

He stole his arm round her shoulders. Sujata shivered at his touch and the next moment submitted to it as if she'd been waiting for it a long time. She let herself lean into the warmth of his body and gently he encircled her body with his other arm and crushed her in his embrace as if never to let go of her again.